320857

FRED BEAR and FRIENDS
THE NEW

House

This book is

Copyright © ticktock Entertainment Ltd 2007

First published in Great Britain in 2007 by ticktock Media Ltd.,
Unit 2, Orchard Business Centre, North Farm Road,
Tunbridge Wells, Kent, TN2 3XF

author: Melanie Joyce
ticktock project editor: Julia Adams
ticktock project designer: Emma Randall
ticktock image co-ordinator: Lizzie Knowles

We would like to thank: Colin Beer, Tim Bones, Rebecca Clunes, James Powell, Dr. Naima Browne, Millwood Designer Homes, Sunrent Tunbridge Wells, Phillip Norwood

ISBN 978 1 84696 507 4 pbk

Printed in China

Picture credits
t=top, b=bottom, c=centre, l-left, r=right, bg=background
All photography by Colin Beer of JL Allwork Photography except for the following: Shutterstock: 22-23 background, 23cr, 23tl.

Every effort has been made to trace the copyright holders, and we apologise in advance for any unintentional omissions.
We would be pleased to insert the appropriate acknowledgements in any subsequent edition of this publication.

Fred

Arthur

Meet Fred Bear and Friends

Betty

Jess

4

Today is a very exciting day. Fred, Jess, Arthur and Betty are moving to a new house!

They have just had their breakfast. Arthur is looking after the keys to their old house.

Now they have to finish packing everything into boxes.

There is lots to do. "Better get on with it!" says Fred.

5

6

Fred and Jess put plates, bowls and mugs into boxes. Everything has to be carefully packed away.

Oops!

Fred has dropped a plate.

"That is one less thing to carry," says Jess, "but be careful of the sharp pieces, Fred!"

Upstairs, Arthur and Betty finish packing their room.

"In you go, Fluffy," says Betty.

Their bedroom looks huge without anything in it.

Then Bill and Bob arrive.
They are the removal men.

Bill and Bob have come
to take the furniture
and the boxes away.

"Thanks, Bob!" says Betty.

Bill and Bob carry Jess'
chest of drawers to the
van. Jess makes sure she
gets out of the way.

Bill and Bob pack everything into their big removal van.

Even Arthur's bike is in the van.

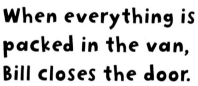

When everything is packed in the van, Bill closes the door.

Now it is time for Betty, Jess, Fred and Arthur to leave their old house behind. They all feel a little bit sad.

13

The van stops.

"Look!" says Betty,

"It's our new home!"

Arthur, Jess and Fred rush to
the window to see.

14

Hurray! There is the estate agent. She gives Fred the keys to the new house.

Fred, Arthur, Jess and Betty can't wait to go inside.

Betty, Arthur, Fred and Jess explore their new house. It is very exciting!

"Wow!"

says Betty, "This is our new bathroom!"

"**Fred!**" calls Jess, "Come and look! Our new garden even has a swing!"

It is time to bring in the furniture and boxes.

Bill and Bob carry everything in from the van. Fred tells them where to put it all.

At last everything is in the new house.

Bill and Bob say "Goodbye."

Fred, Betty, Arthur and Jess have their first dinner in their new home.

That night they all
go to sleep in their
new bedrooms.

Good night, Betty.

Good night, Jess.

Good night, Arthur.

Good night, Fred.

Good night, new home!

21

The new address

Fred, Jess, Arthur and Betty have moved to a new house. This means they have a new address. This is how they remember their new address.

By air mail
Par avion

This is our house number. It is number 4.

This is our post code. It helps the postman find our road.

This is the name of the road we live on. It is called Blossom Road.

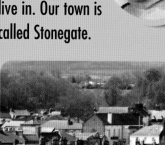

This is the name of the town we live in. Our town is called Stonegate.

Fred, Jess, Arthur and Betty Bear,

4, Blossom Road

Stonegate

ST2 5YP

Can you say your address?

23

The way home

This is a map of Stonegate. Can you help Fred find the way from his old home to his new one?

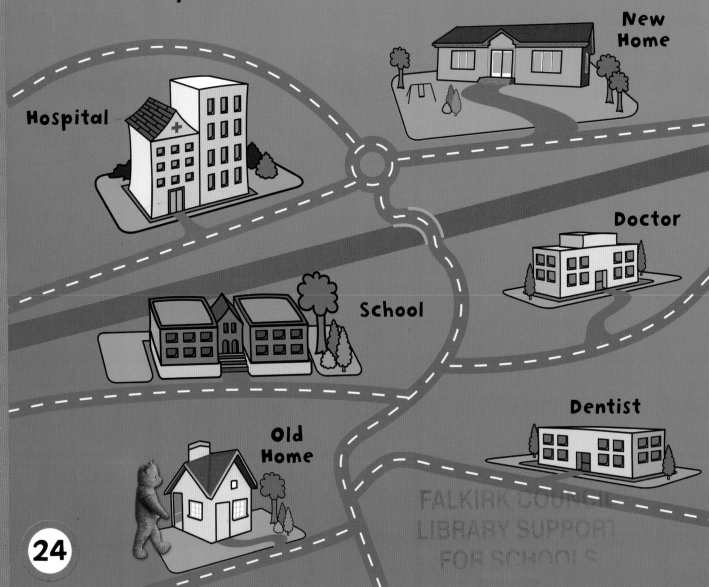

New Home

Hospital

Doctor

School

Dentist

Old Home